P9-DCF-045

WALT DISNEY'S

CINDERELLA

Retold by CYNTHIA RYLANT

Pictures by MARY BLAIR

Disney PRESS

New York • Los Angeles

For C and R, with Love
— C.R.

ACKNOWLEDGMENTS

Front and back cover illustrations are from The Walt Disney Animation Research Library. Page 27: courtesy Kevin Blair; page 28: courtesy Tony Fucile; page 30, page 44: courtesy Howard Lowery; page 52: collection of Eric and Susan Goldberg. All other artwork not attributed to individual collectors is from The Walt Disney Animation Research Library and The Walt Disney Photo Library.

Copyright © 2015 Disney Enterprises, Inc. All rights reserved. Published by Disney Press, an imprint of Disney Book Group. No part of this book may be reproduced or transmitted in any form or by any means, electronic or mechanical, including photocopying, recording, or by any information storage and retrieval system, without written permission from the publisher. For information address Disney Press, 1101 Flower Street, Glendale, California 91201.

Printed in Malaysia
First Edition, 2007
1 3 5 7 9 10 8 6 4 2
Library of Congress Control Number: 2014935031
ISBN: 978-1-4847-1247-4
H106-9333-5-14304

Hand lettering based on Walt Disney's *Cinderella* by Leah Palmer Preiss

Reinforced binding
Visit www.disneybooks.com

Cinderella

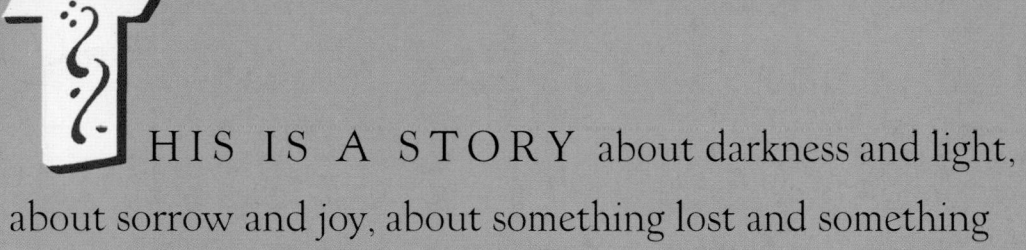

HIS IS A STORY about darkness and light, about sorrow and joy, about something lost and something found. This is a story about Love.

Cinderella was a young and lonely girl, with no father to protect her, no mother to nurture her, and no dear sister with whom she could share secrets.

She lived a dark life in a dark house, with people who did not love her. Each morning when she rose up from bed, Cinderella felt this darkness all around her. Still, she always went to her window and made a wish for her life. Cinderella looked out toward the world that stretched far and away from her small dark room, and she wished for one thing only: Love.

Every day Cinderella wished for Love.

Cinderella's house and Cinderella's life were ruled by a cold, hard woman with a face of stone and a heart sick with envy. This woman hated anything beautiful: the small yellow birds in the trees, the soft rabbits in the gardens, even the roses that bloomed in the summer fields. And she hated Cinderella most of all.

Many years before, Cinderella's mother had died. Cinderella's father married again, not knowing his new wife's unkind heart would in time bleed the life from his own. He died, leaving Cinderella to survive alone. Leaving her with nothing but her beauty and a wish for Love.

Cinderella's stepmother banished her from the warm parts of the house to the cold quarters of the scullery, where Cinderella cooked and cleaned and sometimes cried and sometimes dreamed. She did her duty, she kept her silence. But underneath it all, she was waiting. She had not given up on Love, and she was waiting for it to somehow, somewhere, find her.

Cinderella's two stepsisters also waited in that house, though they waited for something altogether different. They waited for riches. They wanted nothing else. Their hearts were as cold as their mother's, and only wealth had meaning for them. Love meant nothing, and if Love ever did come to them, it is unlikely they would even have known what it was. Like the roses, which did not bloom across their doorways, Love itself did not ever linger.

One day into these lives came something unexpected, something momentous. It was news which would affect the destiny of each of them, in ways none could yet imagine.

The king who ruled their kingdom was growing old. His hair was white. His joints ached. It was time to let go of his throne.

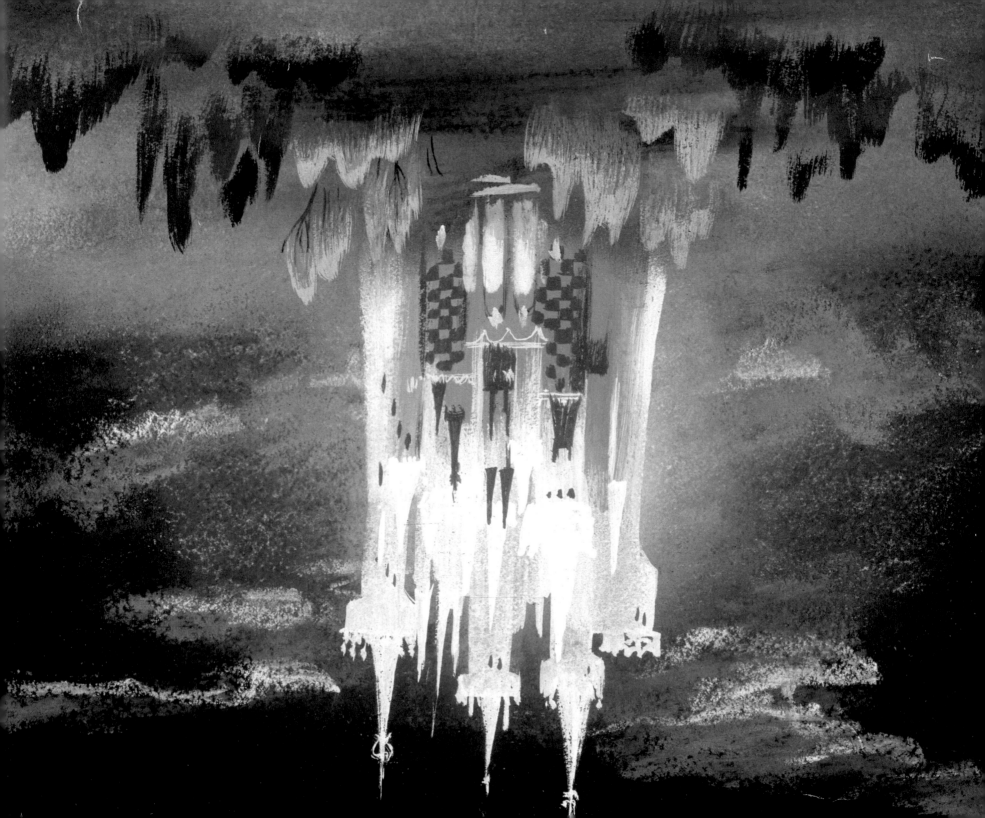

The king had a fine son, a son with integrity and courage and loyalty and honor. The young prince had every quality anyone could ask of a man who would someday be king. The prince lacked only one essential thing. He lacked a wife.

The prince had no wife because he had not yet fallen in love. Any young maiden in the kingdom could have been his, for he was brave and kind and destined to be king. But of all the girls he had ever known or seen, not one touched his heart. Not one moved him.

The king, impatient with his romantic and lonely son, decreed that it was time. Time for marriage. Love is an afterthought, an indulgence, said the king. Love is unnecessary. Find a bride. Make her queen. That will do.

Word spread across the land and into every home that sheltered a young maiden who dreamed of one day being a princess and next day a queen. The king had invited everyone in the kingdom to a grand ball at the palace so that from among them, his son, the prince, might find the young maiden who would become his wife.

Cinderella's stepmother and stepsisters received this news with black longing in their hearts. The stepmother was certain one of her two daughters would be chosen as the future queen. She had, in fact, always thought herself rather queenly. Surely her daughters had learned something from their mother.

No one spoke to Cinderella, of course, about the ball. Servants do not dance at palaces, and they certainly do not become queens.

No one bothered with Cinderella.

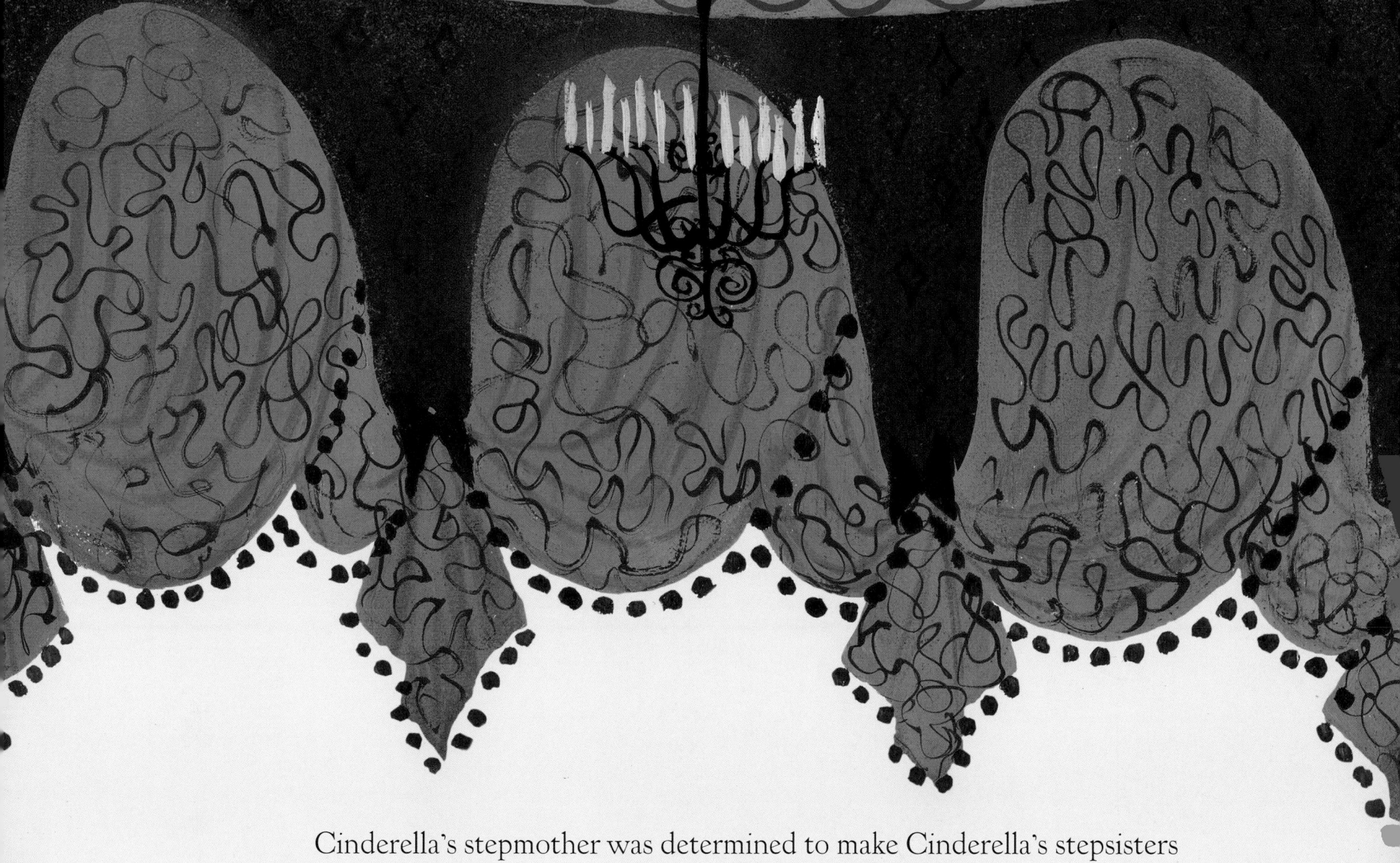

Cinderella's stepmother was determined to make Cinderella's stepsisters attract great attention at the palace. She made them practice their curtsies, their "pleases," and their "pardon me's." And she insisted they refine their musical skills. The lessons were disastrous but completed nevertheless.

THE NIGHT of the grand ball arrived, and Cinderella's stepsisters —their greedy minds swirling with images of gold and silver, of diamonds and rubies, of all they imagined they might possess—departed with their mother for the king's palace.

Cinderella knew when they left the house, why they left the house, and what they were seeking. And she knew something more. She knew, somehow, that she was meant to go to the king's ball as well. Her heart told her. Her heart said that Love was waiting there. Cinderella stared at the sad, shabby, sooty girl in the mirror, and her heart broke for what she dreamed of and could not have.

She could not bear the coldness of the dark house. She went outside and wept.

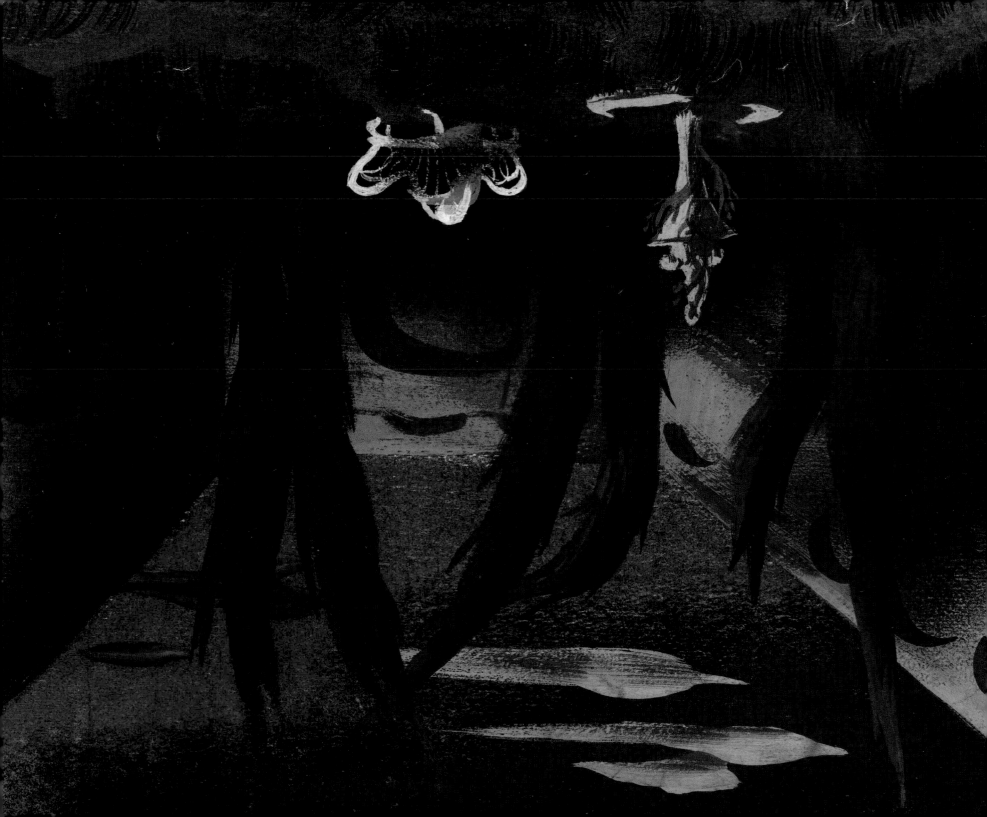

Tears have a wondrous magic about them. They often change everything. And for Cinderella, on this night, tears created a miracle.

A luminous creature appeared beside Cinderella, a heavenly creature, a fairy godmother. The kind and gentle fairy stroked Cinderella's long hair. And she said, "I am here, my dear." Cinderella's tears then flowed like a fountain, now for joy, not sadness. She was an orphan no more.

Cinderella did not have to tell her fairy godmother what she longed for. She did not have to ask for anything at all. Those things which were meant for her found her. A pumpkin in the garden became a coach. Four mice in the grasses became horses. And a child of rags became a vision.

Cinderella went to the ball with a promise to return home at midnight before all the magic went away.

Who can say by what mystery two people
find each other in this great wide world?

How does a young man find his maiden? His heart leads him. He finds her in a room. He asks her to dance. And when he touches her, he knows.

Cinderella and the young prince
danced into a private world all their own.
They did not even speak.

In silence, *Love* found them.

AND WHEN THE HOUR of midnight rang throughout the palace and Cinderella remembered her promise, she took one last look at the prince's face, and she ran. The magic would soon return a pumpkin to its garden and four mice to their grasses and a beautiful girl to the ashes.

Cinderella ran. As she did, one of her slippers fell off and remained on the palace steps behind her.

The prince, surprised and hurt, tried to stop her, but she ran so fast and people were standing in his way. The girl was gone; the only thing left of her a smooth glass slipper.

A YOUNG MAN knows what he must do when the girl he loves disappears. He must find her.

The following day, and days after that, a duke, sent out on order from the palace, traveled the kingdom far and wide with a glass slipper in his hand.

He went to every home in the land,
searching for the foot meant for the shoe
and the heart meant for a prince.

Cinderella waited as she scrubbed the scullery floor. She waited to see if Love would find her. Finally the duke arrived at the house of a cold woman, her two covetous daughters, and her sad and ragged stepdaughter, Cinderella. The duke tried to slide the rough foot of each sister into the glass slipper. Neither fit. One foot was too wide, the other too long, and nothing short of a knife could make them any different.

"Are these the only maidens in this house?" the duke asked the bitter woman who would not, after all, be mother to a queen.

"There is a dirty servant girl somewhere," answered the woman. "You don't want her."

"Very well," said the duke, and he turned to go.

Just then, a shy maiden appeared at the top of the stairs. It was Cinderella.

"May I try on the slipper?" she asked.

The duke, moved by the sincerity of her voice, stopped. He looked at her.

"Come, my child," he said.

Cinderella met him at the bottom of the stairs. But just as the duke reached for her hand, there came the sickening sound of shattered glass. The slipper had fallen to the floor.

"Oh, no!" cried the duke. "The slipper!"

Cinderella looked into the duke's anguished eyes. "I have another," she said softly.

Indeed she did. And as the duke held a second glass slipper in his hands, her lovely foot slid perfectly in.

Cinderella returned to the palace
where Love had always been waiting,
and the prince took her in his arms.

hey lived happily ever after.

The End